DREAMING
★★ OF WAR ★★

BRANDON T. MATHERNE

PALMETTO
P U B L I S H I N G
Charleston, SC
www.PalmettoPublishing.com

Copyright © 2024 by Brandon T. Matherne

All rights reserved
No portion of this book may be reproduced, stored in a retrieval system, or transmitted in any form by any means–electronic, mechanical, photocopy, recording, or other–except for brief quotations in printed reviews, without prior permission of the author.

Paperback ISBN: 9798822963948
eBook ISBN: 9798822968660

DREAMING
★★ OF WAR ★★

In loving memory of Eva.

Author's Note:

To the reader, as you read you may notice something about the chapter titles. Yes, they are song titles, and yes, I am a big Metallica fan. I wanted to come up with a way to make the story feel more impactful, and I believe that the music will help you understand the underlying theme of the book. Thank you, and I hope you enjoy reading it as much as I enjoyed writing it.

TABLE OF CONTENTS

Chapter One: Blackened 1

Chapter Two: The Thing That Should Not Be 7

Chapter Three: The Frayed Ends of Sanity 11

Chapter Four: Creeping Death 17

Chapter Five: Harvester of Sorrow 25

Chapter Six: Some Kind of Monster 33

Chapter Seven: Through the Never 39

Chapter Eight: The Unnamed Feeling 43

Chapter Nine: All Nightmare Long 51

Chapter Ten: Until It Sleeps 57

CHAPTER ONE

BLACKENED

Property of Corporal Ellias J. Cook
1st Battalion Lancashire Fusiliers,
Charlie Company
26 June 1916

"We have arrived at our desired destination in Somme, near Beaumont-Hamel. It is quite a beautiful area, and a shame that a conflict must occur here. Out in the distance, I can see most of the landscape already torn apart by the Germans, bloody bastards. Barbed wire is strewn all over the fields, and their trenches are heavily fortified. I hope we can make a difference here. Our French allies over in Verdun are being bled dry, and our operation will hopefully bring them some relief."

Ellias takes a deep, meditative breath and vents out the stress building up within him.

"My dreams are becoming more…eccentric, but it is the same dream that I keep recalling. I can only recollect fragments of it, a land filled with smoke and fire, after I awake with beads of sweat trickling down my forehead. I know I mustn't worry, but I cannot help but feel something gnawing… clawing…no, slithering, in the back of my mind, wanting to tether itself to my very conscience."

Ellias closes his diary and stows it away in his haversack. Sitting inside the trenches of the British front line, Ellias nervously lets out a long sigh. Writing in his diary helps calm him down, but he can't help but sit here and contemplate what is to come. In a haggard stare, Ellias catches a glimpse of self-reflection within an unusually meager puddle.

He watches as his skin becomes paler with every profound heartbeat pummeling against his sternum as if something deep within him is screaming to be let out. His dark-brown hair contrasts heavily with his paleness and the vivid green and gold colors of his hazel eyes. Ellias runs his hands across and around his chin, feeling for the steadily growing stubble and grasping onto some sense of reality to ensure he is still real.

In his gaze, though, and for a brief moment, the puddle darkens into an abysmal void, and whisps of black ichor trail off with the wind. Petrified by curiosity, Ellias gazes further into this anomaly, and it feels like something is staring back at him, along with faint whispers flowing into his ears. The thunderous sound of cannons abruptly firing shook Ellias as he quickly turned his head toward the sound and then back to the puddle to see whether whatever was there was still haunting him. His concentration is broken by the immediate follow-up of his brothers-in-arms rushing to their positions and their boots crashing through what little water was left in that shallow hole. A pair of boots stops in front of him; Ellias looks up to see the smirking face of his Aussie comrade, Sergeant Edward Sykes, glaring at him.

"Up to it, Cook! The strafe started, and you don't want to miss out on bringing hell to the Huns!"

Ellias shouldered his weapon and rushed down the trench line. As he was making his way to meet up with the rest of the unit, Ellias could hear the explosions of the shells from the Howitzers, striking the ground rhythmically. *This must be what the drums of war sound like,* he thought to himself as he felt the percussive sounds of the artillery in tandem with one another. After sifting through the trenches, cluttered with ammunition casings and iron rations, Ellias meets up with Sergeant Sykes.

"Cook, take up the perisher!"

Ellias handles the periscope propped up against the trench wall, the top half of which just barely raises above the parapet. All he can see are clouds of smoke, debris, and hints of white phosphorus throughout the fields and the German trench line. The fields have become scarred, deformed, and singed from the artillery, creating a land betwixt the two fronts that no man would dare cross.

"It certainly looks like hell on earth out there, Sarge," Ellias reports to Sykes.

"Aye, Cook, that's the point!" Sykes kneels next to Ellias and places his hand on Ellias's shoulder, "I know you weren't there with us in Africa, but believe me, the Huns deserve what's coming to them."

"I would agree with you there, Sarge," Ellias responds, understanding that their operation here could help tip the war in their favor, even if it means they must raze what is left of this beautiful land.

Sykes lets out a short but roaring laugh. "Ah-ha! Damn straight!" he says, slapping Ellias's shoulder. "I'll take it from here, Corp. Go on and report for training. Show 'em a thing or two while you're at it."

Ellias begrudgingly gathers his gear and heads off, the narrow trench winding ahead of him like a serpent through the desolation. The walls, reinforced with wooden beams and sandbags, are damp from the constant moisture that seems to seep into everything. The trench is barely wide enough for two men to pass without brushing shoulders, forcing Ellias to hunch his body as he moves. His pack scrapes against the rough walls, snagging on jutting splinters or stray nails. Every step feels laborious as he navigates through the maze of duckboards, careful not to lose his footing on the slick wood or plunge into the mud below.

At times, the trench narrows even further, constricting like a vice. Ellias has to press himself against the wall to let another soldier pass by, their faces exchanging brief glances filled with exhaustion and the unspoken weight of war. The trench, though meant for protection, feels more like a prison. The sky above, a thin strip of gray, is barely visible between the lips of the trench, making the world beyond feel distant and unreachable. As Ellias continues down the winding path, the walls seem to close in, the air feeling heavier with each passing step. The monotony of the trenches grates on his nerves, but he forces himself to keep moving, ignoring the aches in his back and legs from the awkward, stifling march.

Every so often, he passes a dugout, the narrow entrances carved into the sides of the trench where soldiers huddle together for rest or to escape the relentless artillery fire. The men inside are either silent, their eyes glazed over, staring at nothing as the war grinds on above their heads, or hollering at each other over a round of cards. Everyone has their own way of dealing with stress, as Ellias's is writing.

The day flies by, Ellias exhausting himself from the rigorous training. The comforting thought of sleep rests within his mind as he finds a spot to nest himself inside the trench. Slowly closing his eyes and letting the heaviness take over his body, he drifts into a deep slumber.

CHAPTER TWO

THE THING THAT SHOULD NOT BE

An empty void, vacant of any other life, unoccupied and uninhabited. There are no stars in the sky, no light to cleanse the darkness, and no earth to feel beneath his feet. Nothing. Ellias aimlessly wanders, curious if he could find something from nothing. Surprised, he comes across what appears to be a set of stairs, transparent yet somehow visible in this abyss.

The stairs lead upward, farther into the blackness of the void, where nothing can be seen, yet Ellias continues trailing up the stairs. Each step he takes resonates throughout the void, but he hears no echo, leaving him to believe that this expanse must be infinite.

Ellias walked up what must have felt like hundreds of steps until he suddenly became overwhelmed by a flash of white light that faded into something he was more familiar with. He was back in Somme but stood upon a blackened ground filled with charred wood and soot. Flames engulfed the environment around him, and the once beautiful land that Ellias would seldomly gaze upon was now twisted and malformed into a land of horror.

Ellias steeled himself and pressed on, perhaps in search of something, but for what he was unsure. His mind beckons him forward, and he obeys, keeping a steady pace. As desolate as his surroundings seem, Ellias is surprised by what he discovers and comes to an immediate halt of his own free will, regaining the movement of his legs. Yet he stumbles back and tries to scurry away from what stains his eyes.

A lone tree within this hellfire landscape is somehow still standing, as it certainly was not untouched by the fire that has consumed everything else around it. Hanging from it is a human figure, seemingly strung up by the remains of a parachute. Ellias steadily recovers himself as he attempts to inspect further.

As he got closer, Ellias could make out the uniform of a German soldier, but the remains of the body appeared to be horribly disfigured. The skin no longer exists, burned away by the flames, leaving only patches of charred flesh to cover the sharp and angular features of a skull. The jaw remains attached only by the sinew that spreads throughout the skull like a web, desperately trying to keep whatever is left together.

Ellias leans in closer, without fear of being burned by the flickering fire, becoming disturbingly within reach of the body. He reaches up to feel for the uniform, which is somehow unscathed, but as soon as his hand makes contact, the figure latches onto Ellias's forearm. The bony, fleshless hand takes hold of Ellias with unnatural strength as he grits his teeth from feeling his muscles contort and his bones buckle under the sheer pressure coming from the grip. A moment passes, and the pain becomes numb as Ellias manages to unclench his jaw and open his eyes only to become face to face with this eldritch being. The hollowed eyes of the macabre figure slowly become brimmed with fire; a voice beckons to Ellias as he becomes entranced, and unutterable whispers begin to fade in. Ellias begins to feel his own eyes scorching in pain as if the interior of his skull had combusted and the flames were trying to escape, screaming in agony as his eyes become ablaze and turn into ash, and with that, he is jolted awake from his nightmare.

CHAPTER THREE

THE FRAYED ENDS OF SANITY

30 June 1916

"It came to me again a few nights ago and far more intensely than I can remember. I know dreams are just figments and fabricated realities within the confines of my mind, but the lucidity I experienced made it all feel so…real. I found myself back in the trenches, yet they were altered, twisted into a grotesque parody of their usual state. The walls seemed to breathe, pulsing with a malevolent life of their own. The sky above was a sickly green, swirling with unnatural clouds that seemed to form impossible shapes and symbols. I cannot shake the feeling that this nightmare was more than just a product of my weary mind. It felt like a warning, a premonition of the horrors yet to come. The

line between reality and madness grows ever thinner, and I fear what lies beyond it."

Ellias set down his journal, the weight of the nightmare still pressing heavily on his mind. He rubbed his temples, trying to dispel the lingering whispers that seemed to echo in the corners of his consciousness. The dim light of dawn began to creep into the trench, casting long shadows that danced like phantoms.

He took a deep breath and stepped out of his dugout, the familiar sounds and smells of the Somme greeting him: the distant rumble of artillery fire, the murmur of his comrades preparing for the day's duties, and the ever-present scent of mud and decay. Yet everything felt tinged with an unnatural edge, as if the veil between his nightmare and reality had been thinned.

"Morning, corp," a voice called out, snapping him from his reverie. It was Private Harris, one of the few men Ellias considered a friend in this hellish place. Harris's face was weary, with dark circles under his eyes, speaking to his own restless nights.

"Morning," Ellias replied, forcing a semblance of normalcy into his tone. "How are the rations looking?"

Harris shrugged, handing Ellias a tin cup of lukewarm tea. "Same as always. Piss poor and barely enough to keep us standing, but it'll have to do."

As Ellias sipped the bitter tea, he couldn't help but glance around the trench, half-expecting to see the charred landscape of his dream or the skeletal figure lurking in the shadows. He shook his head, trying to focus on the here and now.

"Cook," Harris said, his voice dropping to a conspiratorial whisper. "You look like you've seen a ghost. Another bad dream?"

Ellias nodded, not trusting himself to speak. Harris was one of the few who knew about the nightmares, though Ellias had never shared the full extent of the horrors he witnessed in them.

"Just try to keep your head on straight," Harris advised. "Command's got something big planned for tomorrow. We need every man ready and focused."

Ellias finished his tea and handed the cup back to Harris. "I'll be ready," he said, more to convince himself than his friend.

The day dragged on, each moment a struggle to keep the nightmare at bay. Ellias threw himself into his duties, repairing fortifications, checking supplies, and doing anything to keep his mind occupied. But every so often, a flicker of movement in the corner of his eye or a stray whisper on the wind would send a chill down his spine, reminding him that the darkness was never far away, something always watching.

As the sun began to set, casting deepening shadows into the trench, Ellias found a moment of solitude. He leaned against the rough wooden wall, staring up at the darkening sky. The stars began to appear, pinpricks of light in the vast expanse, a stark contrast to the void of his nightmare.

"Corporal Cook," a voice broke through his thoughts, but this time it was not Harris. It was Lieutenant Barker, a stern but fair officer who commanded their section of the trench. "I need you to scout ahead. There have been reports of movement in no man's land, and we can't afford any surprises tonight."

Ellias nodded, steeling himself for the task. As he gathered his gear and prepared to venture into the treacherous expanse, the whispers from his nightmare echoed in his mind. He pushed them aside, focusing on the mission. The line between reality and madness was thin, but he knew he had to hold it together—for his sake and the sake of his comrades.

He crawled out of the trench and into the eerie twilight of no man's land, every sense on high alert. The landscape was a twisted maze of barbed wire, craters littered with the dead, and shattered remnants of war. Ellias moved cautiously while keeping his head as low as possible, each step a reminder of the fragile boundary between his waking world and the horrors that lurked just beyond.

As he scouted ahead, a feeling of unease settled over him, stronger than the usual tension of being in enemy territory. The air felt thick, almost palpable, and the distant sounds of battle seemed muffled as if he were moving through a dream once more.

In the distance, he saw movement—a shadowy figure flitting between the wreckage. He signaled back to the trench, indicating potential enemy activity. As he crept closer, the figure came into clearer view and a cold dread washed over him. It was not an enemy soldier but something else entirely, something that should not exist in the waking world.

The figure turned toward him, its eyes burning like the ones from his nightmare. The whispers began anew, more insistent, more maddening. Ellias froze, his mind racing. Was this real or another figment of his fractured psyche?

Before he could decide, the figure vanished into the shadows, leaving Ellias alone once more. He quickly returned to the trench, his report concise but suggesting that what he saw was just a trick of the moonlight and leaving out the details of the eerie figure. The line between reality and nightmare had blurred once again, and Ellias knew that his struggle against the encroaching madness would require all his willpower.

CHAPTER FOUR

CREEPING DEATH

The hours crept by, and dawn approached once more, bringing with it a sense of grim determination. Ellias sat in his dugout, meticulously checking his equipment. The memory of the shadowy figure from the previous night still gnawed at him, but he forced himself to focus on the task at hand. Today would be crucial—a creeping barrage movement to push farther into the German line.

"All right, lads, gather 'round," Lieutenant Barker's commanding and steady voice cut through the morning air. The company assembled, bunched up and shoulder to shoulder around what the troops had started calling "The Pit," the tension palpable as they awaited their orders.

"We've got a big push today," Barker began. "First wave, you will be moving forward under a creeping barrage. The artillery will lay down a curtain of shells ahead, and you will advance behind it, trailing a distance of approximately fifty yards. Timing is everything. Move too slow, and you'll be caught in the open. Move too fast, and you'll be caught by our fire. So stride on at a steady pace."

Ellias nodded along with the others, absorbing the instructions. The plan was simple in theory but deadly in execution. The operation's success depends on their ability to stay coordinated and maintain the pace.

"Sergeant Sykes, you'll lead your section," Barker continued, turning his head to meet with the sergeant's eyes. "Make sure they stay in line and move with the barrage."

Sykes, his demeanor as tough as ever, nodded. "Will do, sir."

"Good. We'll move out in fifteen minutes. Make your final preparations."

Ellias swiveled his head, glancing at the men around him, who were already checking their rifles and gear. He could see the fear in their eyes, mirroring his own. But there was also a grim determination, a shared understanding of what needed to be done.

"Stick close to Ellias and match his pace; he'll be up front," Sykes instructed. "Keep your heads down and follow the movement. We'll cover the sides and make sure we don't lose anyone."

The minutes ticked by, each one stretching into an eternity, when suddenly, the ground beneath Ellias trembles violently, shaking loose clods of dirt from the trench walls. A deafening roar erupts in the distance, so powerful that the air itself seems to shudder. Ellias instinctively drops to a knee, gripping the edge of the trench for balance.

A massive explosion that thunders across the battlefield. Even from his position, miles away, Ellias can feel the shockwave roll through the earth, a force so immense that everything becomes silenced within its presence. The very air feels charged with raw energy as if the world itself has been ripped open.

A towering plume of smoke and debris rises into the sky like a dark monolith, twisting and boiling in the distance. The blast carves a massive crater into the enemy line, a deep, gaping wound in the earth. For a brief moment, everything is silent, as though the world is holding its breath, before the sky is filled with the sound of artillery fire once more.

Ellias feels the pressure in his ears, the ground still rumbling beneath him as dirt and debris rain down on the trench. The soldiers around him are wide-eyed, some muttering curses under their breath as they struggle to comprehend the scale of the explosion. The stench of ammonal and smoke mixes with the ever-present smell of death, creating a sickening miasma that clings to his throat.

Finally, the signal came, and the first shells began to fall, a deafening roar that shook the earth. The barrage moved forward in a steady line, and Sergeant Sykes signaled for the advance.

The men climbed out of the trench and into no man's land, the air stagnant with smoke and the acrid smell of explosives. The ground a churned-up mess of mud and debris, making every step a struggle. They pressed on, the relentless rumble of the barrage guiding their way.

Ellias kept his eyes on Sergeant Sykes, who expertly maneuvered his section through the chaos. The artillery shells explode just yards in front of them, sending plumes of dirt and shrapnel into the air as they try to navigate through the openings of the barbed wire. The initial advance went according to plan, but they were unaware that the Germans were ready for them.

Without warning, German machine guns erupted from their positions, their high-velocity rounds stitching through the air, creating a deadly tapestry of chaos and demise across no man's land. The crackles of the bullets were staggering, a relentless staccato that instilled fear into the hearts of every unfortunate soul that stood within that forsaken land. Bullets whizzed past, and the first casualties fell among the section. Men dropped to the ground, their cries lost in the cacophony of war.

Sergeant Sykes shouted over the din, trying to coordinate their response, but the heavy fire was overwhelming.

Ellias crouched low, his heart pounding as he moved to assist a wounded comrade reaching out for help. Ellias looked down and realized it was Harris, with a bloodied hand pressed over his chest. Ellias quickly rips a piece of cloth from his undershirt, raises Harris's hand to place it on his wound, and heavily presses Harris's hand back down.

"Keep it tight, okay?" Ellias exclaimed, looking into his friend's fading eyes; then he took a firm grip on his comrade's uniform collar and began to pull.

"Take cover!" Sykes bellowed, signaling for his section to fall back. The order was almost lost in the roar of the battlefield, but the men responded quickly, scrambling to find any shelter they could.

They headed toward the nearest tree line, a small forested area that promised some respite from the relentless fire. The advance turned into a frantic scramble as they dashed across the exposed ground. The barrage was still active, but its effectiveness waned under the intensity of the German counterattack.

Ellias reached the tree line, dragging an injured Harris with him. The trees, though offering some cover, were thin and sparse, providing only minimal protection. The gunfire was sporadic but intense, and the area quickly became a chaotic scene of men huddled behind whatever cover they could find.

"Report!" Sykes's voice cut through the chaos. He was moving between his men, checking for injuries and assessing their situation.

Ellias, panting and covered in mud, said, "Help! I need help!" Ellias attempted to examine the wound but was caught off guard by Harris's coughing, and speckles of his blood landed on Ellias's face. Right then, Ellias knew Harris was dying. He struggled to breathe as he choked on his own blood; a bullet pierced his lung. With Harris in his arms, Ellias tries to swaddle his head and bring him some sort of comfort as his last moments come to an end. Harris struggles to hand Ellias a picture, and just as Ellias takes it from him, his arm collapses to the ground. Trying to see past the smeared blood, Ellias notices that the picture is of Harris's family. Knowing that Harris was his mother's firstborn son, as he is sure that most men here are, he hopes to write to Harris's mother and let her know that her son did not die alone.

Ellias surveys the chaos surrounding him. The section had suffered heavy casualties, and several men were either dead or gravely wounded. The once-tight formation had fractured under the pressure, and now they face the grim task of regrouping and holding their position.

"We can't stay here," Sykes said, his voice grim but resolute. "We need to get some distance from the enemy's fire and find a better defensive position. Keep your heads down and stay sharp." Sykes placed a hand on Ellias's shoulder. "Let him go, mate."

Ellias nodded, his thoughts racing. The familiar fear from his nightmares seemed to seep into the present reality, blurring the lines between the two. The constant barrage of enemy fire and the sight of fallen comrades made it hard to focus, but he knew that survival depended on their ability to adapt and fight through the chaos. He took a deep breath, laid Harris's head down on the ground, and closed his eyes, steeling himself for the next phase of the assault. The battle was far from over, and the horrors of the day had only just begun.

With Sergeant Sykes leading the way, Ellias and the remaining members of his section prepared to push forward once more, determined to hold their ground and press on despite the overwhelming odds.

CHAPTER FIVE

HARVESTER OF SORROW

The initial respite provided by the cover was brief, as the intense German fire had only temporarily relented. With their casualties accounted for and their positions reorganized, the men were ready to move once more.

"Eyes sharp, men," Sykes barked. "We're pushing on to the German trenches. Stay close, keep low, and watch for enemy positions."

Ellias nodded, his heart pounding with a mix of fear and determination. Harris's death had reemerged from the nightmare that had haunted him and still lingered at the edges of his mind, but he forced himself to focus on the task at hand. The creeping barrage had moved ahead, creating a moving wall of explosions that provided some cover but also threatened to turn the battlefield into a maelstrom of death.

The men advanced cautiously, stepping over fallen comrades and debris. The once-muddy ground was now a churned-up quagmire dotted with craters and shattered remnants of war. Each step was more difficult than the previous, and the noise of battle precluded any semblance of normalcy.

As they moved forward, the German defenses came into clearer view. Barbed wire entanglements and concrete bunkers marked the enemy positions, and the occasional burst of machine gun fire reminded them of the dangers that lay ahead.

Ellias kept close to Sykes, who led with a steady hand and a keen eye. Despite the chaos, the sergeant maintained a calm demeanor, barking orders and ensuring that his section remained coordinated. The men followed his lead, moving in tight formation and staying alert for any signs of enemy resistance.

As they neared the German trenches, the intensity of the fire increased. The enemy was well prepared, their guns blazing from well-fortified positions. Ellias and his section had to navigate through a gauntlet of bullets and shrapnel, their progress slowed by the overwhelming opposition.

"Covering fire!" Sykes shouted, signaling for his men to provide suppressive fire while the rest of the section moved forward. The crackle of rifles and the stutter of machine guns filled the air, creating waves of sound reverberating throughout the battlefield.

Ellias took his place in the line, firing at any movement he could see through the smoke. His hands were steady, but his mind raced with the surreal echoes of his nightmare. The burning, skeletal figure from his dream seemed to haunt every shadow, every corner of the battlefield.

Despite the barrage of fire and the growing number of casualties, they pushed on, inching closer to the enemy trenches. The ground became even more treacherous, littered with obstacles and the craters left by the artillery fire. Each advancement was a battle in itself, as they fought both the terrain and the German defenses.

Finally they reached the edge of the German trench line, where the fighting became more brutal and personal. The enemy was determined to hold their ground, and the trench itself was a labyrinth of dugouts and barricades. Ellias and his men had to fight their way through, clearing out enemy positions and securing the area.

The battle was fierce, a chaotic clash of soldiers in close combat. Ellias moved with grim determination, his rifle a constant companion as he fought to gain ground. The nightmare's echoes seemed to fade in the face of the immediate danger, replaced by the adrenaline and focus required for survival.

Ellias and Sykes pushed up to a German-occupied machine gun bunker in an attempt to clear it out. Sykes pulls out a "Mills bomb," ejects the pin, and chucks it into the bunker, followed by a deafening explosion and shrapnel ricocheting off the concrete. The bunker was silent, its occupants either dead or driven away. The smell of spent ammunition and burning metal was heavy. Ellias moved forward with Sykes to inspect the area, their rifles at the ready.

Suddenly, from the shadows of the bunker, a lone German soldier emerged, his hands raised in surrender. The soldier's face was pale and fear-stricken, his uniform tattered and stained. He looked exhausted and terrified, the weight of the battle evident in his eyes.

"Nicht schießen!" the German soldier cried out, his voice trembling. "Ich gebe auf! Ich gebe auf!"

Don't shoot! I surrender! I surrender!

Sykes and Ellias exchanged a glance. Neither of them could understand German, but they recognized the non-verbal communication of surrender. The sight of the surrendering soldier was unusual amid the chaos, and the decision on how to handle him was complex. Sykes moved forward cautiously, his expression grim.

"Stay! Put!" Sykes slowly ordered, his voice firm as he signaled with his hand for the German to get down. "We'll deal with you in a moment." The German soldier complied and fell to his knees, his hands behind his head with his fingers interlaced.

Ellias's mind raced. The soldier's plea for mercy seemed almost surreal in the midst of the violence. As the reality of their situation pressed down on him, the echoes of his nightmare seemed to merge with the present. The charred, skeletal figure from his dream appeared to loom at the edges of his vision, the line between hallucination and reality blurring.

Ellias took a step closer to the German soldier, trying to process the situation. The soldier's pleading eyes and outstretched hands seemed to mock the futility of their struggle. Ellias felt a chill creep over him, a sense of dread that he couldn't shake. The whispers from his nightmare seemed to seep into his thoughts, urging him toward a path of madness.

"Bitte," the German soldier continued, his voice breaking. "Ich möchte einfach nur leben. Ich möchte zu meiner Familie zurückkehren. Bitte, töte mich nicht."

Please, I just want to live. I want to return to my family. Please, don't kill me.

Only this time, it wasn't German that Ellias heard. Instead, maddening whispers penetrated his mind, uttering words that could not be comprehended. However, he could make out a single command hidden between the whispers.

Kill…Kill…KILL!

Ellias blinked, and suddenly the surrendering German soldier resembled the appearance of the skeletal creature from his nightmare. Ellias's grip tightened on his rifle. The surrealness of the situation, combined with his own slithering fear, made it hard to think clearly. The soldier's desperate pleas seemed to echo the whispers from his dreams, a distorted reflection of his own fears and insecurities.

In a sudden, uncontrollable surge of panic, Ellias raised his rifle and fired. The shot rang out, and the German soldier fell, his body collapsing to the ground. The echo of the gunfire seemed to resonate through the trench, mingling with the sounds of distant explosions and the cries of battle.

Sykes looked on in shock, his eyes wide as he processed what had just happened. The men around them fell silent, their expressions a mix of confusion and horror.

"Ellias! What the hell—" Sykes began, but his words were cut short by the severity of the situation.

Ellias stood frozen, his mind an anarchic whirl of guilt and fear. The soldier's pleading eyes haunted him, a stark reminder of the madness that had overtaken him. The boundary between reality and the nightmarish visions he had been experiencing seemed to have shattered, leaving him adrift in a sea of despair as he dropped to his knees.

"For Christ's sake, get it together, Ellias!" Sykes snapped, his voice harsh but laced with concern. "More Germans are coming!" Sykes grabbed Ellias by the forearm and yanked him upward. "WE! ARE! LEAVING!"

Ellias nodded numbly, trying to pull himself back from the edge of madness. He turned away from the fallen soldier, focusing on the task at hand. The battle raged on, and the fight for survival continued. But the moment of insanity had left a deep scar on his soul, a reminder of the darkness that lurked not only on the battlefield but also within himself.

As they moved forward to consolidate their position, Ellias's thoughts were consumed by the memory of the soldier's final moments. The echoes of his nightmare seemed to blend with the horrors of war, leaving him to grapple with the haunting realization that the true enemy might be the madness that lies within.

CHAPTER SIX

SOME KIND OF MONSTER

The weight of his actions hung heavily on Ellias as the remnants of their section regrouped in the captured trench. The German soldier's lifeless eyes seemed to follow him, a foreboding reminder of his actions. Sergeant Sykes, his face a mask of scarcely contained fury, approached Ellias with purposeful strides.

"What in God's name were you thinking, Ellias?" Sykes snarled, grabbing Ellias by the collar and shoving him against the trench wall. "That man was surrendering! He was no threat!"

Ellias could see the anger in Sykes's eyes, but his own mind was still clouded with the echoes of his nightmare. He struggled to find the words to explain the fear that had driven him to such a harrowing act.

"I—I don't know, Sarge," Ellias stammered, his voice shaking. "I saw something, felt something. It was like a nightmare come to life. I couldn't control it."

"Nightmares? We're living in a fucking nightmare, and we still follow orders!" Sykes spat, his grip tightening, using every bit of willpower to hold back from striking Ellias. "We can't afford to lose our heads out here, Ellias! Not now, not ever!"

Before Ellias could respond, the sound of approaching footsteps and muffled voices reached their ears. Sykes released him and turned to the men, his eyes scanning the horizon. The tension in the trench was palpable, the silence broken only by the distant rumble of artillery.

"Get ready!" Sykes barked, raising his rifle. "Incoming!"

The German counterattack came swiftly, their soldiers emerging from the smoke and shadows like phantoms. Gunfire erupted, and the trench was quickly engulfed in panic. Ellias and Sykes took cover, firing back at the advancing enemy.

The battle was fierce; the Germans were determined to reclaim their lost ground. The men in Ellias's section fought valiantly, but the sheer number of the enemy proved overwhelming. Ellias watched his comrades fall one by one, their screams of pain mingling with the ringing roar of gunfire.

Amid the chaos, Ellias found himself fighting side by side with Sykes. Despite their tension, they moved with determined coordination born of necessity. The trench became a hellish battlefield, debris flying into the air as bullets crackled by their heads.

Ellias fired his rifle until it clicked empty, then he scrambled to reload as the Germans pressed their attack. He saw Sykes fighting fiercely, his face set in a hell-bent snarl. The sergeant's presence was a steadying force, even in the thick of the nightmare.

"Ellias, on your left!" Sykes shouted, pointing to a group of German soldiers attempting to flank them.

Ellias swung his rifle around and fired, the shots finding their marks. The Germans fell, but more took their place, their relentless advance pushing Ellias and Sykes to the brink.

The trench was littered with the bodies of the fallen, both friend and foe. The stench of death was oppressive; the cries of the wounded became a haunting backdrop to the battle. Ellias felt his resolve waver, the weight of his actions and the horrors of the battlefield threatening to crush him.

"We need to fall back!" Sykes yelled, his voice barely audible above the chaos. "We can't hold this position!"

Ellias nodded, his mind a whirlwind of fear and adrenaline. Together, they retreated through the trench, firing at the pursuing Germans. The world around them was a blur of smoke and blood, the veil between reality and nightmare growing ever thinner.

As they reached a more defensible position, Sykes turned to Ellias, his expression grim. "We're the last ones left, Ellias. We've got to hold out until reinforcements arrive."

Ellias swallowed hard, the reality of their situation sinking in. The two of them, alone against the oncoming tide of German soldiers. The odds were bleak, but a newfound determination tempered the fear in Ellias's heart. He couldn't let his comrades' sacrifices be in vain.

The Germans renewed their assault, and Ellias and Sykes fought with desperate ferocity. Every shot and every movement was a struggle for survival. The nightmarish visions that had plagued Ellias seemed to merge with the brutal reality of the battle, the shadows of his mind blending with the horrors around him.

Time lost all meaning in the chaos. Ellias fired until his fingers were numb, reloaded until his hands bled. The Germans pressed closer, their numbers seemingly endless. But through it all, Sykes stood firm, his presence a beacon of strength in the darkness.

"Stay with me, Ellias!" Sykes shouted, his voice hoarse. "We're not done yet!"

Ellias gritted his teeth and nodded, drawing on the last reserves of his strength. They fought on, two soldiers against the tide, their determination unyielding. In the face of overwhelming odds, they held their ground, refusing to give in to the madness and the fear.

The night dragged on, the battle a relentless onslaught of violence and death. Ellias felt his sanity fraying at the edges, the eldritch whispers of his visions growing louder. But he pushed them aside, focusing on the fight, on the need to survive.

As dawn began to break, the German assault wavered, then broke, their soldiers retreating under a commanding order. Ellias and Sykes slumped down in the trench together, battered, bloodied, and broken.

The trench was a scene of devastation, the ground littered with the dead and dying. But for now they had survived. Ellias looked at Sykes, his eyes filled with a mixture of exhaustion and gratitude.

"We made it," he said, his voice barely a whisper.

Sykes nodded, his expression menacing but relieved. "Aye, we made it. But this war's far from over, Ellias. Stay sharp, and don't lose your head again. I can't afford to lose you."

Ellias nodded, the weight of his actions and the horrors of the battle still heavy on his mind. The nightmare was far from over, but for now they had won a small victory. As the first light of dawn illuminated the battlefield, Ellias resolved to face whatever horrors lay ahead with valor.

CHAPTER SEVEN

THROUGH THE NEVER

The dawn light filtered with frailty through the branches of the trees that were still standing, casting an eerie glow over the battlefield. Ellias and Sykes, exhausted and bloodied, trudged their way through the carnage and aftermath of the battle and took refuge in a shallow dugout. The trench was eerily quiet now, the sounds of battle replaced by the groans of the wounded and the cries of the dying.

Ellias collapsed against the dugout wall. His body ached, and his strength faltered from the events of the past hours. He closed his eyes, hoping for a moment's respite from the horrors that had unfolded. But as sleep claimed him, it brought no peace.

Ellias found himself back in the desolate void, the same emptiness that had haunted his previous nightmares. The ground beneath him was cold and unyielding, a stark contrast to the environment he had been in before. Darkness pressed in from all sides, a palpable force that seemed to invade his very soul.

He wandered aimlessly, the silence oppressive and all-consuming. The void began to take the shape of the trenches previously held by the Germans. As he walked, the memories of the moment before the battle played out in his mind: the German soldier's pleading eyes, the sound of the gunshot, the lifeless body crumpling to the ground.

A soft whisper broke the silence, a voice that seemed to come from everywhere and nowhere at once. "Ellias…"

He turned, searching for the source of the voice, but saw only darkness. The whisper grew louder, more insistent, as if it were coming from within his own mind. "Ellias…you cannot escape your sins…"

Panic gripped him as the voice continued, its tone both mocking and sinister. "You are a murderer, Ellias. You killed in cold blood. You are no better than the enemy you fight."

"No!" Ellias shouted, his voice echoing through the void. "I didn't mean to…it wasn't me…"

The darkness seemed to close in around him, the voice growing louder and more distorted. "You cannot hide from the truth. You are doomed to madness, just as you are doomed to this endless void."

Ellias stumbled, falling to his knees. The ground beneath him felt like ice; the chilling embrace crawled up his limbs, sapping his very soul. He could feel the weight of his actions pressing down on him, a crushing burden that threatened to break him.

Suddenly the void shifted. The darkness gave way to a twisted version of the battlefield, a nightmarish landscape of fire and ash. The bodies of his fallen comrades littered the ground, their eyes staring accusingly at him. The air filled with the stench of death and decay.

In the center of this hellish scene stood a tall, shadowy figure of a man draped in a black cloak with strands of black ichor wisping from it. The shadow slowly turned to Ellias and said, "You cannot escape your fate, Ellias. You are marked for madness, chosen by the void."

Ellias tried to stand, but his legs felt like lead. He could only watch in horror as the shadow approached. With each step it took, Ellias could catch a glimpse of an aberrant, malformed entity of crawling chaos before it reverted back to its shadowy form. Its dark hand reached out; the touch was ice-cold, sending a jolt of fear through Ellias's body.

The shadow's face twisted into a grotesque grin. "Join us, Ellias. Embrace the madness. Embrace the void. Embrace ME."

Ellias screamed, the sound ripping through the fabric of the dream. He felt himself falling, plunging into the darkness that swallowed him whole. The ground gave way beneath him, and he plunged into an abyss of swirling shadows and whispers.

As he fell, the voice of the eldritch being grew louder, echoing in his mind. "You are ours, Ellias. You will never escape. You will never find peace."

The abyss seemed to stretch on forever, an endless descent into madness. Ellias's mind reeled, the boundaries between the world he knows and the abyssal void merging into a conjunction of horror, a relentless assault on his sanity.

When he finally jolted awake, his body was drenched in sweat, his heart pounding in his chest. The dugout was dimly lit from the dawn's light, the sounds of the battlefield a distant memory. He could hear Sykes's steady breathing nearby. The sergeant's presence was a small comfort in the darkness.

Ellias took a deep breath, trying to steady his racing thoughts. The nightmare had been so vivid, so absolute. He could still feel the icy touch of the shadow's hand, could still hear the whispers.

He knew that the horrors he had faced on the battlefield were far from over. The true battle was within his own mind, a struggle against the madness that threatened to consume him. As he lay back, Ellias stared up into the ceiling of the dugout, refusing to close his eyes again.

CHAPTER EIGHT
THE UNNAMED FEELING

"Yesterday, we fought tooth and nail against the German counterattack. Sykes and I are the only ones left from our section. The rest...the rest are gone, taken by the relentless tide of war, and Harris...I could not do anything to save him. I can't shake the guilt, the overwhelming sense that their deaths are on my hands. But we must press on. I must press on. For their sake, for Sykes, and for my own sanity. This war is far from over, and the true battle lies within."

Ellias paused, his pencil hovering over the page. He glanced over at Sykes, who was still asleep, his face lined with exhaustion. The sergeant had been a rock amid the chaos, a source of strength and resolve. Ellias took a deep breath and continued writing.

"I owe Sykes my life. Without him, I would have been lost long ago. He sees the madness creeping in—I know he does—but he hasn't given up on me yet. I can't afford to give up on myself either—not now."

★ ★ ★

As Ellias finished his entry, Sykes stirred and opened his eyes. He looked over at Ellias, his expression a mix of concern and determination.

"Ellias," Sykes said, his voice rough from sleep. "You're up early."

Ellias closed his journal and nodded. "Couldn't sleep. The nightmares…they're getting worse."

Sykes sat up, rubbing a hand over his face. "I figured as much. You've been through hell, Ellias. We both have. But we can't let it break us."

Ellias sighed, the weight of his guilt pressing down on him. "I killed that German soldier, Sykes. He was surrendering, and I just…it was almost like I wasn't myself. I can't get it out of my head."

Sykes leaned forward, his gaze steady. "War does terrible things to a man's mind. I've seen it before. You're not the first, and you won't be the last. But you need to focus, Ellias. We need to figure out our next move."

Ellias nodded, appreciating Sykes's pragmatism. "What do we do now? We're cut off from the rest of the company, and our section is gone."

Sykes took a deep breath, thinking. "First we need to assess our situation. See what supplies we have left and find a way to link up with the rest of the company. If we stay here, we're sitting ducks."

Ellias stood and began checking their packs, taking stock of their remaining ammunition, rations, and medical supplies. Sykes did the same, the two of them working in a silent, efficient rhythm.

"We've got enough to last a couple of days," Sykes said finally. "But we need to move soon. The Germans will be regrouping, and they'll want to reclaim this line."

Ellias nodded. "I can scout ahead and see if there are any safe routes. I could maybe find a way to the rest of our lines."

Sykes shook his head. "We stick together. You're in no shape to be wandering off alone, and we're stronger as a team. We'll move cautiously, and we'll find a way through."

Ellias felt a surge of gratitude for Sykes's unwavering support. Despite the horrors they had faced, the sergeant's resolve remained unbroken. It gave Ellias a sliver of hope, a memento that they could still make it through this nightmare.

As they packed up their gear, the trench seemed to close in around Ellias, the walls a constant reminder of the violence that had taken place. The memories were fresh, the screams and gunfire still echoing within his thoughts.

"Ellias," Sykes said quietly, breaking the silence and pulling Ellias away from his thoughts. "We've…both seen things no man should ever see. But we have to keep our heads. We have to be strong."

Ellias looked at Sykes, seeing the strain in his eyes. "I'll do my best, Sykes. I promise."

With their packs secured and weapons ready, they climbed out of the dugout and began their cautious advance. The morning mist clung to the ground, shrouding the battlefield in an eerie ambiance. The distant rumble of artillery was a constant reminder of the ongoing conflict, but for now, the immediate area was quiet.

They moved through the trenches, stepping over the bodies of fallen soldiers, their eyes scanning for any sign of movement. The devastation was immense, the ground scarred and broken by countless explosions.

Sykes led the way, his movements precise and controlled. Ellias followed closely, his senses heightened by the lingering fear. Every shadow seemed to hide an enemy, every sound a potential threat.

As they reached a section of the trench that offered a better vantage point, Sykes raised his hand, signaling for Ellias to stop. They crouched low, peering over the edge. The landscape before them was a wasteland pockmarked with craters and littered with debris.

"We need to find higher ground," Sykes said, his voice barely above a whisper. "Get a better view of the area. See if we can spot any of our troops."

Ellias nodded, his eyes scanning the horizon. "There's a small rise over there," he said, pointing to a hill in the distance. "If we can make it, we might be able to see more."

Sykes glanced at the hill, then back at Ellias. "All right. We move quickly and stay low. Keep your eyes peeled."

They set off toward the hill, moving from cover to cover, their footsteps silent on the soft earth. The tension was palpable, and every moment was a test of their nerves. As they climbed the rise, the view expanded, revealing the full extent of the battlefield.

From their vantage point, they could see the scattered remnants of the British line, pockets of soldiers holding out against the German defensives. The scale of the conflict was staggering, the sheer number of lives lost a sobering reminder of the war's brutality.

"There," Sykes said, pointing to a group of British soldiers hunkered down in a makeshift defensive position.

"That's our best bet. We make for them, link up, and figure out our next move."

Ellias nodded, his resolve strengthening. "Let's go."

They began to descend from the hill; however, Ellias felt a strange sensation wash over him. The air thickened, almost suffocatingly so, and the sounds around him became muffled as if he were underwater. He shook his head, trying to clear it, but the feeling only intensified.

Suddenly the battlefield around him seemed to come to life in a way that was both familiar and horrifying. He could see soldiers moving, shouting orders, and firing their weapons, but they weren't real. They were echoes—spectral images of men long dead, replaying their final moments in an endless loop of violence and despair.

Ellias froze, his breath catching in his throat. The figures moved around him, oblivious to his presence. A British soldier staggered past, his chest riddled with bullets, blood spraying from his wounds. Another man screamed in terror as a German soldier bayoneted him, and his screams turned into desperate attempts to breathe from the blood clogging his throat, the horror etched into his face as he fell to the ground.

"Ellias!" Sykes's voice cut through the haze, sharp and urgent. "Ellias, you with me?"

But Ellias couldn't move. His eyes were locked on the visions before him, his mind unable to separate the echoes from reality. He could feel the madness creeping in, the same darkness that had plagued his dreams now invading his waking hours.

Sykes grabbed Ellias by the shoulders, shaking him roughly. "Ellias, listen to me! Whatever it is that you're seeing is not real! You need to focus!"

Ellias blinked, his vision clearing slightly. The echoes began to fade, but the fear lingered, a gnawing presence at the back of his mind. He looked at Sykes, his face pale and drawn.

"I saw them, Sykes," Ellias whispered, his voice trembling. "I saw them all. The dead…they're still here."

Sykes's grip tightened. "They're not real, Ellias. It's just your mind playing tricks on you. We need to keep moving."

Ellias nodded weakly, the images still burned into his memory. "I'm trying, Sarge. I'm trying."

"Good," Sykes said, his tone firm but understanding. "We're almost there. Just keep it together a little longer."

With Sykes guiding him, Ellias forced himself to move, though every step felt like he was wading through quicksand. The echoes of the dead still lingered at the edges of his vision, but he focused on Sykes, using the sergeant's steady presence as an anchor to reality.

CHAPTER NINE

ALL NIGHTMARE LONG

Ellias shook his head, the whispers growing louder in his mind. "It's them. The echoes. They're following us, hunting us down."

Sykes's face hardened. "There's nothing there, Ellias. Focus. We need to move."

But Ellias couldn't focus. The whispers were growing more insistent, pulling at the edges of his sanity. He could see shapes in the trees, shadows that shouldn't be there, watching him, waiting.

"Ellias!" Sykes snapped, grabbing his arm. "We don't have time for this. We need to go. Now."

Ellias blinked, snapping back to reality. The shadows faded, and the whispers receded, but the fear remained. He nodded shakily, forcing himself to stand. "I'm…I'm okay. Let's go."

They continued moving, pushing through the underbrush as quietly as possible. The forest was eerily silent, the usual sounds of nature replaced by an oppressive stillness. Ellias's heart pounded in his chest, every nerve on edge as they neared the enemy line.

As they approached the clearing that marked the edge of the forest, Sykes held up a hand, signaling for Ellias to stop. He peered through the trees, his eyes narrowing as he spotted movement ahead.

"There," Sykes whispered. "Looks like a German patrol."

Ellias followed his gaze, his grip tightening on his rifle. A small group of German soldiers was moving through the clearing, their weapons at the ready. They were too close for comfort but hadn't spotted Ellias and Sykes yet.

Sykes glanced at Ellias, his voice barely audible. "We can't engage them here. Too risky. We need to find another way around."

Ellias nodded, though the tension in his body was unbearable. Every instinct screamed at him to attack, to fight. Ellias felt a familiar sensation creeping over him—the same oppressive presence he had felt during his nightmares. The eldritch being was near, watching him, feeding off his fear and anxiety.

His breath quickened, his vision blurring as the forest around him began to twist and warp. The trees stretched into grotesque shapes, their branches reaching out like claws. The ground beneath his feet seemed to pulse with a sickening rhythm.

"Ellias, what's wrong?" Sykes's voice cut through the haze, but it sounded distant, distorted.

Ellias couldn't respond. The whispers were back, louder and more insistent than ever. They filled his mind, drowning out all other thoughts. He could see the shadows moving again, closing in around him, their shapes growing clearer with each passing second.

They weren't just shadows. They were the dead, the echoes of the soldiers he had seen before. Their faces were twisted in agony, their eyes empty and hollow. They reached out to him, their mouths moving in silent screams.

"Ellias!" Sykes's voice was more urgent now, but it was too late.

The echoes engulfed Ellias, their cold hands gripping and pulling him down into the darkness. He could feel the eldritch being's presence, its malevolent power washing over him, consuming him.

He was losing his grip on reality, slipping further into the abyss. The line between the real and the unreal blurred, and the horrors of the battlefield merged with the terrors of his mind. The soldiers within the German patrol group were replaced with images of the monstrosities Ellias was seeing. All of a sudden, out of sheer fear and with an unexpected feral snarl, Ellias lunges forward, his sanity finally shattering under the weight of the eldritch influence. He broke from cover, charging at the German patrol with wild, frenzied movements.

"Ellias, no!" Sykes shouted, but the roaring in Ellias's ears drowned out his voice.

The Germans turned, their eyes wide with shock as Ellias barreled toward them, rifle swinging. Before they could react, he was upon them, his rifle butt slamming into the first soldier's head with a sickening crunch and his helmet flying off into the distance.

Ellias didn't stop. He couldn't stop. The voices were in full control now, driving him into a blood-fueled frenzy. He struck again and again, each blow fueled by a primal terror and rage that consumed him. Sykes let off rounds from his rifle in an attempt to assist Ellias, but it was pointless.

The German soldiers tried to fight back, but they were caught off guard by the ferocity of Ellias's assault. One by one, they fell under his relentless onslaught, their blood staining the earth.

Sykes grabbed Ellias, trying to wrestle him away from the last soldier. "Ellias, stop! You're going to get us both killed!"

Ellias hesitated, his vision clearing for a brief moment. He saw Sykes's face, saw the fear and desperation in his eyes. But then the eldritch presence surged again, and the whispers drowned out everything else.

With a guttural scream, Ellias wrenched free of Sykes's grip and slammed his rifle down on the last German soldier, who had been trying to crawl away. The soldier cried out, but Ellias was beyond mercy. He brought the butt of the rifle down again and again, until the soldier's bloodcurdling screams were silent.

Sykes tackled Ellias from behind, forcing him to the ground. Panting from the struggle, Sykes pulled back slightly but kept a wary eye on Ellias. His face was a mix of shock, anger, and a dawning realization of the dangerous instability in the man he once considered a comrade. Slowly he reached for his rifle, the weight of what he had to do settling heavily on him.

"Ellias…I'm sorry," Sykes said, his voice shaking slightly as he brought the rifle to bear on Ellias. "You're not yourself. This…this has to end."

Sykes's hands trembled as he pulled the trigger, but there was only a hollow click. He stared at the rifle in disbelief, realizing with horror that he had used the last of his ammunition in the previous fight. Ellias's confusion turned to rage, the whispers flaring up in his mind, urging him on. With a guttural roar, he lunged at Sykes, his hands finding the other man's throat.

Sykes struggled as they both fell to the ground, his eyes wide with terror, but Ellias was beyond reason. The madness consumed him completely as he squeezed, his vision blurring with rage and fear. With a swift outward motion of his forearms, Sykes managed to break Ellias's grip but was swiftly met with a fierce jab from his fist. With Sykes temporarily dazed from the punch, Ellias quickly grabbed Sykes's entrenching tool from his equipment and, with such visceral fear, began to ferociously hack, tearing into the thick flesh of Sykes's neck as blood sprayed across his face and uniform, killing the only man that believed in him.

CHAPTER TEN

UNTIL IT SLEEPS

There was no one left to answer, no one left to share the burden of his guilt. Ellias was alone, surrounded by the bodies of his enemies—and now that of the man he had called a friend.

He stood shakily, his mind a fractured mess of guilt, fear, and the ever-present darkness that had taken root in his soul. He knew there was no going back, no redemption for the horrors he had unleashed.

As he walked away from the carnage, leaving Sykes behind, the whispers in his mind grew stronger once more. Ellias stumbled through the smoke and ruin, his mind a chaotic storm of whispers and screams. The landscape around him was a nightmarish blur of craters, twisted metal, and the broken remnants of men who had once been his comrades—or enemies—it no longer mattered.

He could no longer distinguish between the real and the imagined. The eldritch horror that had taken root in his mind had hollowed him out, leaving behind only a shell of the man he once was. The memories of what he had done, of Sykes's lifeless eyes staring up at him, were like ghosts clinging to his every step, but they no longer elicited any emotion. The madness had numbed him to the core.

Ahead, the British line came into view, the tattered remnants of their forces regrouping, their faces lined with exhaustion and despair. Ellias wiped the blood from his face, smearing it across his uniform as he tried to straighten himself out. He knew he had to appear normal, whatever that meant now. The madness still roiled within him, but he forced it down, burying it deep beneath a mask of weary determination.

As he approached the line, the other soldiers barely glanced at him, their own minds consumed by the horrors they had witnessed. To them, Ellias was just another survivor, another body returning from the carnage. They were too broken to see the madness in his eyes, too shattered to notice the tremor in his hands.

A lieutenant, his uniform caked with mud and blood, looked Ellias over briefly before nodding. "Bleeding Jesus, Cook, you made it," he said, his voice hollow. "We lost a lot of good men, but I'm glad to see you're still with us. Fall in with the others. We're regrouping before the next push."

Ellias nodded, not trusting himself to speak. He moved through the ranks, blending in with the other soldiers, each as haunted as the next. The whispers in his mind had quieted, but they were still there, lurking just beneath the surface.

As he took his place among the ranks, Ellias's eyes scanned the faces of those around him. They were all shadows of their former selves, their spirits crushed under the weight of endless battle. He wondered if any of them felt the same darkness that had consumed him or if they were simply too broken to care.

The line began to move, the soldiers charging forward with grim resolve. Ellias moved with them, one foot in front of the other, his body moving on autopilot. The madness was still there, gnawing at the edges of his mind, but he kept it at bay, knowing that he had to survive—if only to see the end of this nightmare.

As they advanced, Ellias's thoughts turned inward to the creature that had invaded his dreams, the eldritch being that had twisted his mind and driven him to murder. He could feel it still, lurking in the shadows of his consciousness, waiting for the moment to strike again.

The British line continued its relentless advance, the sound of gunfire and explosions growing louder as they neared the front. Ellias gripped his rifle more tightly, his knuckles white as he steeled himself for what was to come. The madness surged within him; he strained to push it down, focusing on the task at hand. He would survive. He had to.

As the first shots rang out and the battle began anew, Ellias was just another soldier among the ranks, a hollow man moving forward in a war that had long since lost all meaning. But deep inside, the eldritch whispers continued, a constant reminder that his battle was far from over and that the darkness within him would hold him forever.